stay fucking motivated.

VERY SWEARY COLORING BOOK

this book belongs to

....

....

....

Fuck
your
comfort
zones.

Ignore
the
fucking
haters.

You were born to fucking shine.

Fuck
your
fear.
Embrace
courage.

Believe
in
your
fucking
abilities.

Fuck fate. Create your destiny.

Make
it
fucking
happen.

Push
your
fucking
limits.

Fuck excuses.
Pursue your passions.

You
are
fucking
fierce.

Fuck
standing
still.
Keep
moving
forward.

Focus
on your
fucking
comeback..

I am
my best
fucking
investment.

Fuck settling for less.

Rise
and
fucking
shine.

Dare
to
fucking
dream.

Fuck
self-doubt.
Believe
in
yourself.

Unleash your fucking potential.

You
are a
fucking
badass.

Fix your fucking crown.

Believe in your fucking dreams.

Unleash
your
fucking
greatness.

Go fucking do it.

I can
and I
fucking
will.

I will never forget that I am fucking powerful.

Chase dreams, break chains, fucking soar.

Fuck mediocrity. Strive for greatness.

No regrets, just epic fucking adventures.

Stay
fucking
focused.

RISE
LIKE A
FUCKING
PHOENIX

Make your journey fucking legendary.

Stop
talking
and
start
fucking
doing.

Show
people
who
the fuck
you are.

I'm a fucking beast.

If you can dream it, you can fucking do it.

Only stop when you are really fucking tired.

Your fuckups don't define you.

You always have a fucking choice.

Be a
fucking
rainbow in
someone
else's
cloud.

Push
your
fucking
boundaries.

Conquer
your
fucking
destiny.

NO
FUCKING
EXCUSES

Stay fucking relentless.

Keep fucking dreaming.

Fucking
do it
anyway.

Seize
the
fucking
day.

Fuck caring what other people think.

I am
fucking
enough.

I'm
made of
TRUE
FUCKING
GRIT.

Made in the USA
Middletown, DE
25 July 2024

57768381R10057